USBORNE FIRST READING
Level Three

USBORNE FIRST READING

The Three Little Pigs

retold by
Susanna Davidson
Illustrated by Giorgia Overwater

USBORNE FIRST READING

Chicken Licken

retold by
Russell Punter
Illustrated by Ann Kronheimer

USBORNE FIRST READING

The Castle that Jack Built

Lesley Sims
Illustrated by
Mike Gordon

USBORNE FIRST READING

The Dinosaur Who Lost His ROAR

Russell Punter
Illustrated by Andy Elkerton

Once upon a time,
there was a little girl
called Goldilocks.

She had lovely golden hair
and looked as good as gold.

But Goldilocks
wasn't good.

Goldilocks!

She was naughty.

Gold!

She liked to do something naughty every day.

"If you don't stop being naughty," said her mother, "your hair will turn blue."

"I don't believe you!" said Goldilocks, and put salt in the sugar pot.

"If you carry on like this,"
said her father, "you'll grow
warts on your nose."

"I don't believe you!" said
Goldilocks...

...and gave her little
brother a haircut.

"Now," thought Goldilocks.
"What shall I do next?" Then
she remembered the woods.

Her mother always said,
"Don't go into the woods.
They're full of bears."

The woods are
too dangerous!

That made
Goldilocks want to
go there even more.

Goldilocks waited until
no one was watching...

...and crept out through
the back door.

DANGEROUS WOODS

"This is fun!" thought
Goldilocks, as she skipped
down the path.

12

"There aren't any bears here at all."

Goldilocks skipped around a corner and saw...

13

...a pretty little cottage.

Goldilocks knocked
on the door. There was
no answer.

Bear
Cottage

But there was a delicious
smell coming from inside.

"Mmm," said greedy
Goldilocks, walking in.

16

She followed the smell...

...and saw three bowls of
porridge on the table.

"I'm sure no one would notice if I had a tiny taste."

18

First, Goldilocks tried
the great, big bowl.

Next, she tried the middle-sized bowl.

Last of all, Goldilocks tried the porridge in the tiny bowl.

She ate it ALL up.

Feeling full, Goldilocks
looked for somewhere to sit.

First, she tried the
great, big chair. "Too
hard," said Goldilocks.

Next, she tried the middle-sized chair.

Too soft.

Last of all, Goldilocks
tried the tiny chair.

"It's just right,"
thought Goldilocks,
until...

The chair broke.

"Oops!" giggled Goldilocks.

"I'll just lie down instead."

Goldilocks climbed the
stairs to the bedroom.

She tried the first bed.

She tried the second bed.

She tried the third bed.
"Just right!" said Goldilocks.

In no time at all,
Goldilocks was fast asleep.

As she slept, a large,
heavy paw pushed at the
front door.

Three bears
stomped into the house.

There was a great,
big father bear...

a middle-sized
mother bear...

and a cuddly
little baby bear.

Father Bear went straight
to the table. He was hungry.

He looked at his porridge
bowl and let out a great,
big **GROWL**.

"Who's been eating my
porridge?" he said, in his
great, gruff voice.

"Who's been eating *my* porridge?" said Mother Bear, in her middle-sized voice.

"Who's been eating *my* porridge?" squeaked Baby Bear, in his tiny voice.

They've eaten it all up!

Father Bear looked
around the room.

"Who's been sitting in my
chair?" he growled, in his
great, gruff voice.

"Who's been sitting in *my* chair?" asked Mother Bear, in her middle-sized voice.

"Who's been sitting in *my* chair?" squeaked Baby Bear. "They've broken it!"

Then the three bears
heard loud snores
from upstairs.

They climbed
the stairs.

"Who's been sleeping in my bed?" growled Father Bear, in his great, gruff voice.

"Who's been sleeping in *my* bed?" said Mother Bear, in her middle-sized voice.

"Who's been sleeping in *my* bed?" squeaked Baby Bear, in his tiny voice.

She's still there!

Baby Bear began to cry.
He cried so loudly,
Goldilocks woke up.

She looked at the three
bears, opened her mouth
and Screamed.

Goldilocks ran
out of the house.

She ran home as fast
as she could go.

45

USBORNE FIRST READING
Level Four

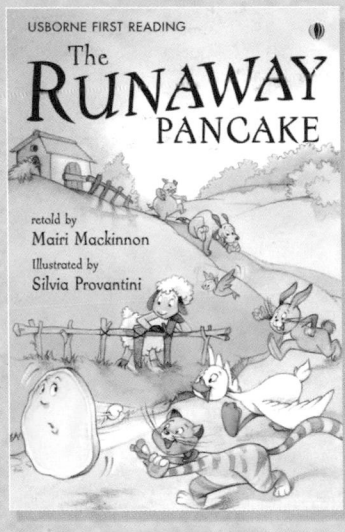